This Book Belongs to:

Mickey's Young Readers Library

VOLUME

5

Scrooge and the Golden Eggs

© MCMXC **The Walt Disney Company.**

Developed by The Walt Disney Company in conjunction with Nancy Hall, Inc.

Story by Diane Namm/Activities by Thoburn Educational Enterprises, Inc.

This book may not be reproduced or transmitted in any form or by any means.

ISBN 1-885222-38-6

Advance Publishers Inc., P.O. Box 2607, Winter Park, FL. 32790

Printed in the United States of America

098765432

One bright spring day, Donald bought a goose for Grandma Duck. It was a very beautiful goose.

As Donald was walking to Grandma's farm with the goose, he didn't notice his nephews, Huey, Dewey, and Louie. They were playing ball beside the road.

"Look," said Huey. "Uncle Donald is carrying a goose."

"It looks like the goose in our book about Jack and the beanstalk!" said Dewey.

"Yes," agreed Louie. "Do you think it lays golden eggs, like the one in the book?" he wondered.

"Probably," said Dewey. "It looks just like that goose."

The boys were so interested in the goose that they didn't hear Scrooge McDuck come up behind them. Scrooge listened to them talking about the special goose and the golden eggs.

"What if it *is* true?" Scrooge asked himself. "If that goose does lay golden eggs, I must have it!"

Scrooge caught up to Donald. "Good morning, Donald," he said in a friendly voice.

"Good morning, Uncle Scrooge," Donald replied.

"My, that's a beautiful goose you have there," said Scrooge.

"Why, thank you," said Donald. "It *is* a lovely bird."

"I'd like to buy that goose from you," said Scrooge.

"Sorry, Uncle Scrooge," Donald replied, "I'm giving it to Grandma."

"Here now, Donald," said Scrooge, "I'll pay you twice what you paid for it. You can buy Grandma another goose."

"You want to give me twice what I paid?" asked
Donald. He was puzzled. Why would Uncle Scrooge
pay him more than the goose was worth? Then he
thought to himself, "Well, it's Uncle Scrooge's
money, after all. He must know what he is doing.
And if I sell him this goose, I can buy two just like it
for Grandma!"

So Donald agreed to sell the goose.

Uncle Scrooge set off for home. Now he had the special goose. Surely soon he would have golden eggs, too!

"Heh, heh, heh," Scrooge laughed to himself. "When this goose lays its golden eggs, I, the richest duck in the world, will be even richer!"

When Scrooge got back to his mansion, he gave the cook and the butler the day off. Then he pulled down all the window shades and locked all the doors. "I wouldn't want anyone else to find out about my goose," he said to himself.

Scrooge set the goose on the floor. Then he waited for the golden eggs. Nothing happened.

"Well," Scrooge said to the goose, "when are you going to start laying some eggs? And I mean some *golden* eggs!"

The goose looked at Scrooge with its bright brown eyes. It gave a soft honk!

Still nothing happened. No eggs appeared.

Scrooge began to get upset. "How do I get this goose to lay eggs?" he wondered. He thought and he thought. Then he said, "I have it! I'll call Grandma Duck. She has a farm. She must know how to make a goose lay eggs."

So Scrooge called Grandma. Without even saying, "Hello," he asked, "How can I get a goose to lay eggs?"

"Why do you want to know about geese, Scrooge?" Grandma asked.

"Please, Grandma, just tell me how," he said.

"Well," said Grandma, "you have to make sure the goose is not too cold . . . not too hot . . . not too hungry. And it needs lots of exercise."

Scrooge wrote down what Grandma told him and quickly said goodbye.

Just then Grandma heard a knock at her door.
It was Donald. He had brought her two beautiful
white geese.

"Why, thank you, Donald," said Grandma. "Isn't
this strange? I was just talking to Scrooge about
geese."

"I guess that's because I just sold him one," said
Donald. "He paid me twice what it was worth."

"Goodness," said Grandma. "It isn't like Scrooge to pay more than a goose is worth. I wonder why he wanted a goose so badly?"

"I don't know," said Donald. "Maybe he wanted some goose eggs for breakfast."

Meanwhile, Scrooge was trying to get the golden goose to lay golden eggs.

Looking at his notes, he read, " 'Not too cold.' Hmmm. Perhaps it is a little cool in here."

So Scrooge set the goose in his favorite chair. He lit a fire in the fireplace and pulled the chair close to the fire. Next he covered the goose with a nice, soft blanket.

Then he sat back to wait for the golden eggs.

The goose began to get warm. It held its wings away from its body. Its feathers started to droop. The goose looked at Scrooge, but it laid not one egg.

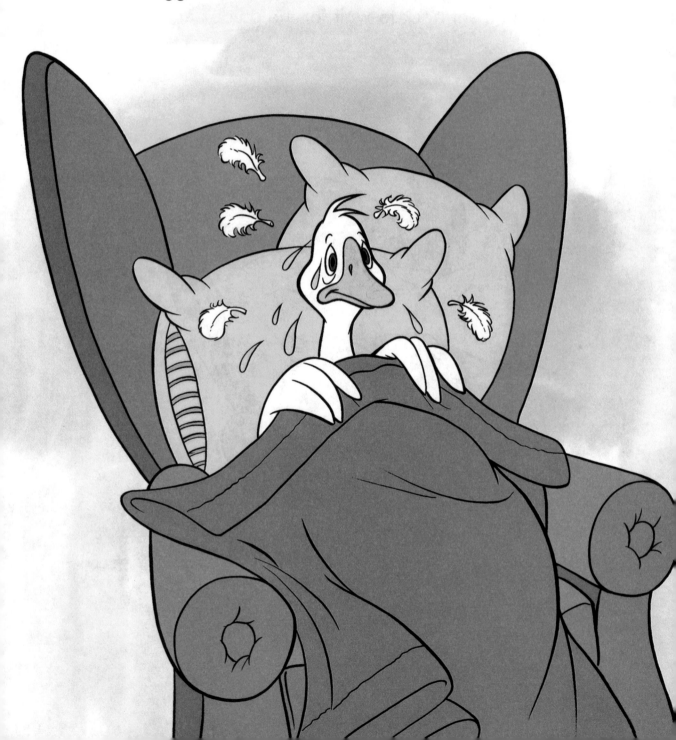

Scrooge was pretty warm himself. He looked at his notes again. He read, " 'Not too hot' . . . oops!"

Quickly Scrooge pulled the blanket off the poor goose. Then he put out the fire and moved the chair away from the fireplace.

Scrooge ran to the kitchen. He returned with a
bag full of ice, and he placed it on the goose's
head. Then he turned on a fan and pointed it right
at the goose.

"There!" he said. "You should be cooler soon."

In no time at all, the goose cooled off. Then it
began to shiver. It fluffed up its feathers. The goose
held its wings close to its sides. Its beak began to
turn blue. But it laid not one egg.

By this time Scrooge had pulled a blanket over
his shoulders to keep himself warm. Again, he read
over Grandma's notes. " 'Not too hungry,' " he read.
"That must be it!"

Scrooge turned off the fan. He took the ice bag from the goose's head. Then he hurried to the kitchen to make some nice hot soup.

"Here you are, goose," he said, setting the soup bowl in front of the goose.

The goose stared at Scrooge with its bright brown eyes. But it did not eat. And it laid not one egg.

"What do I have to do to make you lay eggs?"
Scrooge cried. "I want some of those golden eggs!"
The goose just stared back at Scrooge.
"What else did Grandma say to do?" Scrooge
wondered. "Hmmm. 'Needs exercise.' That's it!"

The next thing the poor goose knew, it was running around outside. Scrooge was running after it. As Scrooge chased the goose he said, "If it's exercise you need, then it's exercise you'll get!"

Finally Scrooge had to rest. So the goose gladly settled down to rest, too. But the goose laid not one single egg.

None of Grandma's ideas had worked. Scrooge couldn't think of anything else to do. How was he to get the golden eggs out of this goose?

Then Scrooge remembered his nephews talking about a book—*Jack and the Beanstalk.* Maybe the secret of the golden eggs was in that book!

Quickly Scrooge went to his bookshelf and took down the book. He opened it to the picture of the goose. Sure enough, the goose was laying golden eggs.

Scrooge ran out to the back yard with the book.
He pushed the picture of the goose laying a golden
egg under his own goose's beak.

"See this!" he shouted. "This is what you're
supposed to do!"

The goose looked at the book. Then it looked up
at Scrooge. The goose blinked its eyes. But it laid not
one egg.

Scrooge looked at the book again. Maybe if he acted a little more like a giant, his goose would act a little more like a goose that could lay golden eggs.

So Scrooge stood up as tall as he could. He read the giant's words from the book: "Lay, goose! Lay!" He used his loudest voice.

The goose began to look very unhappy. It
ruffled its feathers. The goose wasn't used to people
yelling at it in loud voices. It stared straight at
Scrooge. Then it gave a loud honk! But it laid not
one egg.

Scrooge could stand it no longer. "Lay, goose! Lay!" he shouted, jumping up and down, waving his arms.

The goose gave another loud, frightened honk! It flapped its great wings. It took off into the sky. And not one egg had it laid!

Just then Donald came by. "Uncle Scrooge!" he called. "How are you getting along with your new goose?"

"The silly goose flew away!" moaned Scrooge. "And it didn't lay one golden egg!"

"Golden egg?" repeated Donald. "Real geese don't lay golden eggs. That only happens in fairy tales."

Suddenly Scrooge understood how silly he had been. But he didn't want his nephew to know, too. " 'Good old egg,' I said," Scrooge shouted. "It didn't lay one good old egg!"

"Well," said Donald, as he watched the goose disappear in the sky. "I'm sorry you lost your goose, Uncle Scrooge. I'll be glad to get you another one, if you'll give me twice what I pay for it again!"

This was more than Scrooge McDuck could stand. He went back inside his mansion and slammed the door.

"If I hadn't been so greedy," he thought sadly, "I wouldn't have lost my money or my goose."

He began to feel better when he got to his money room. It was the one place that could always make him feel better.

"I may be poorer than I was before," he told himself, "but I'm still the richest duck in the world!"

Think About It

Tell The Story

See how well you remember the story of *Scrooge and the Golden Eggs.* Point to the four pictures below in the order in which they happened.

After your child does the activities in this book, refer to the *Young Readers Guide* for the answers to these activities and for additional games, activities, and ideas.

Act It Out

Show how the goose acted when she was hot.
Show how the goose acted when she was cold.
Show how the goose acted when she was tired.
Show what the goose did when Scrooge yelled at her.

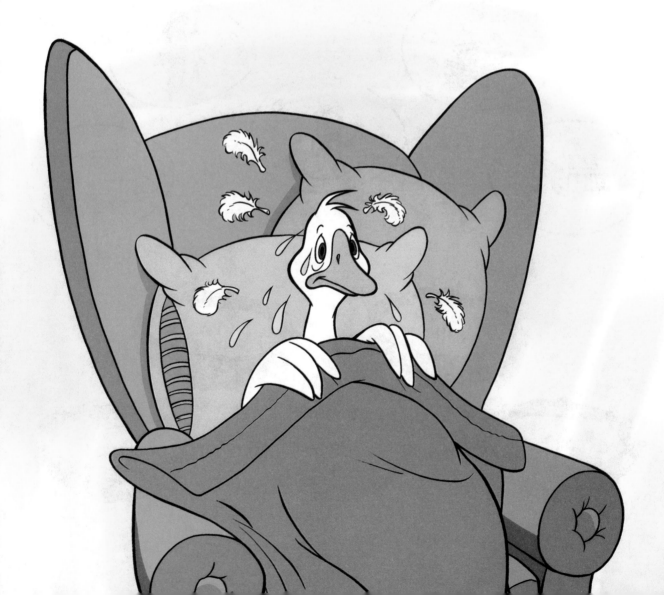

Fun With Words

Which Goes With What?

Read the words on the nests. Match the pictures on the eggs to the words on the nests that best describe each one.

soft

hot

cold

large

loud

Wordmaking

How many words can you make from the letters in GOLDEN EGGS?

(Examples: GO, SOLD, EGG, OLD)

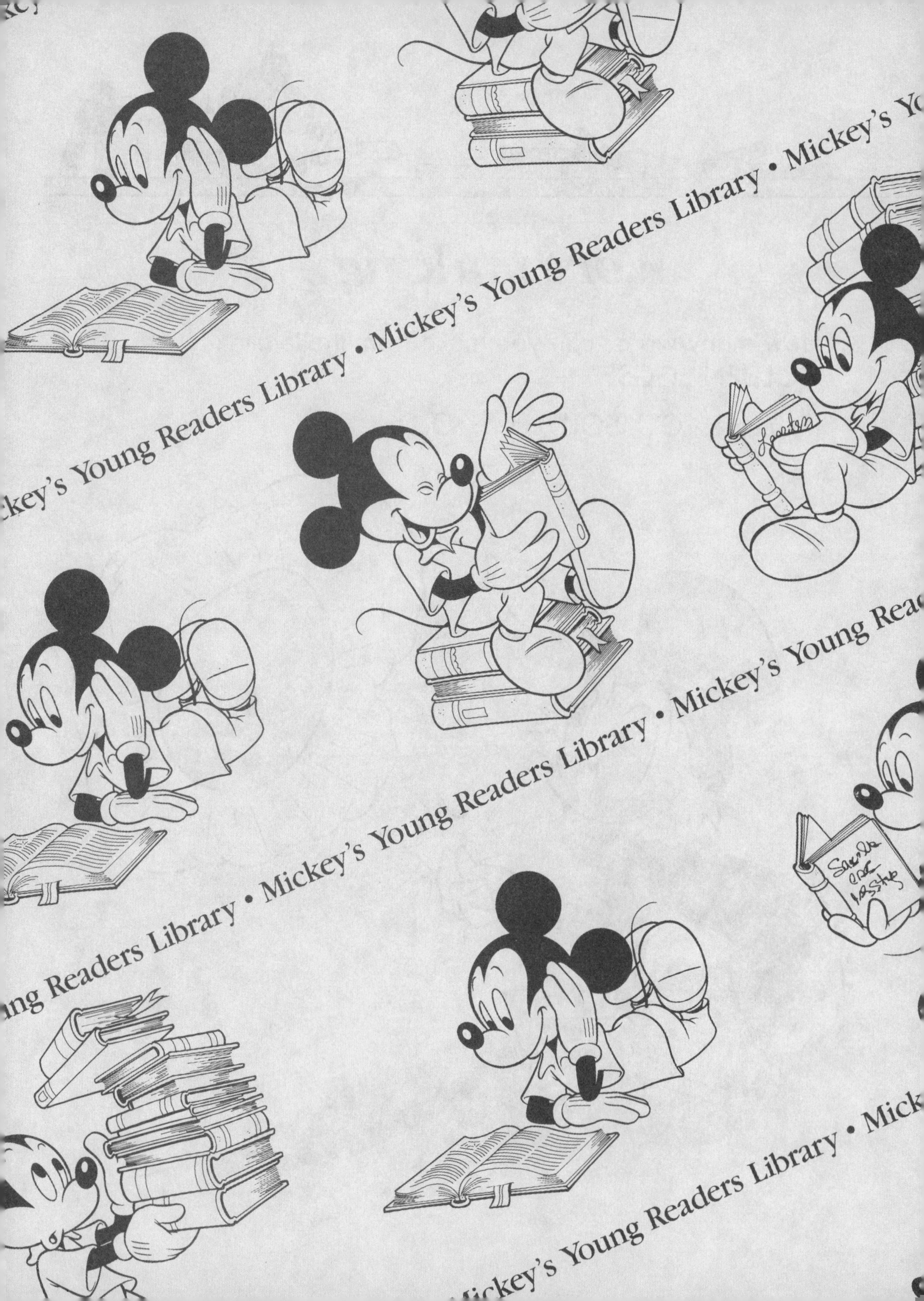